To
Deborah and Guy

THE PIE WAGON

By *LILLIAN BUDD*

Illustrated by MARILYN MILLER

Lothrop, Lee & Shepard Co., Inc.

NEW YORK

An old white horse came down the street
pulling a tall thin wagon

with three little steps
lopping down behind.

With its wiggly wheels squeaking,
  its body creaking,
  the horse's hoofs kept time:
    Clip—clop
    Clip—clop

When he wanted to stop to sell his pies,
the Pie Man shouted, "Whoa!"
He pulled hard on the reins
to make the horse stand still.

The walls of the wagon were lined with racks
   to hold the pies.
   Down the center was a narrow aisle,
   and through this aisle
   the tall thin Pie Man slipped
   to get the pies that people bought,

While the white horse stood still.

The Pie Man
   never ate his pies himself
   for fear he would grow too fat
   to slip through the narrow aisle
   in the center of the skinny wagon.

One day when he called: "Pies! Any
    pies today?"

A little girl named Tilly came
and asked the Pie Man
if she could climb up
into the tall and skinny wagon
to choose a pie for her mother.

And the Pie Man helped her in.
Twenty-six kinds of pie
were arranged on racks
from top to bottom—
starting with A
and going right through
the letters of the alphabet:

a pple

b lueberry

c herry

d ewberry

e gg custard

f ig

24

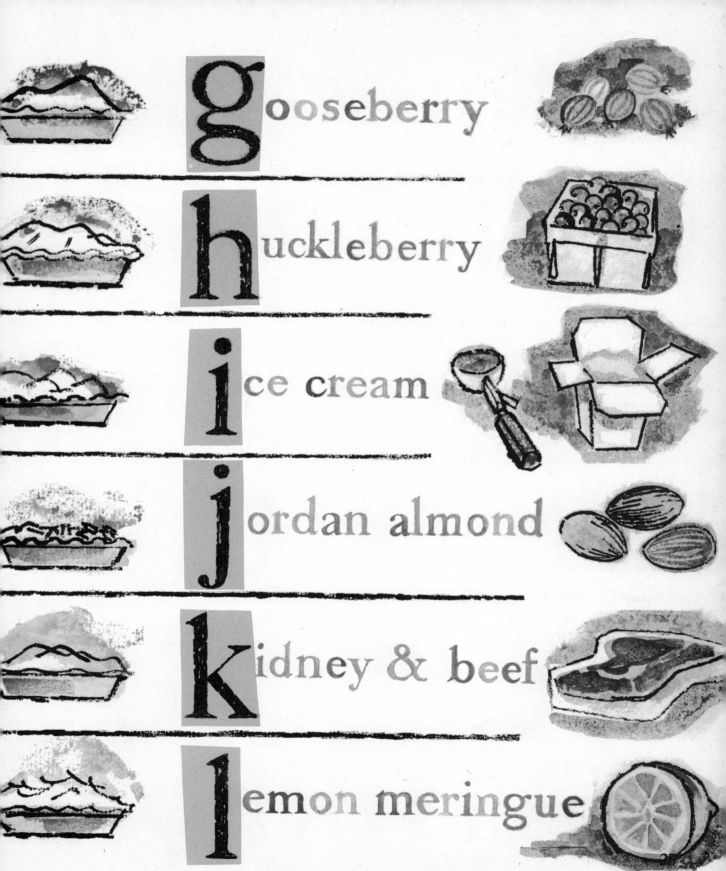

gooseberry

huckleberry

ice cream

jordan almond

kidney & beef

lemon meringue

 **m**ince

 **n**ut

 **o**range cream

 **p**each

 **q**uince

 **r**aisin

Sweet potato

tarts

Up-side down
    pineapple

Vanilla cream

Wild grape

X

 **Y**oungberry

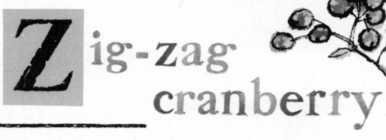 **Z**ig-zag
cranberry

When she looked at the pie in the X rack,
    the little girl was puzzled. There
    was no name for it.
"What's the name of the pie in
the X rack?" she asked.

The skinny Pie Man laughed. "Can
you think of the name of a pie
that begins with X?"

The little girl thought and thought, but she couldn't think of a pie that began with X.

"I couldn't either," said the Pie Man. "So I use this rack for the eX tras— eX tra big and eX tra delicious. Today it's banana cream with strawberries on top."

"Oh," said the little girl. "That's
the one I want!"

And she took it home to her mother.

The Pie Man went back to the driver's seat,
   picked up the reins,
   "clucked" to his horse
   and said, "Giddap, giddap."

U. S. 1132214

35

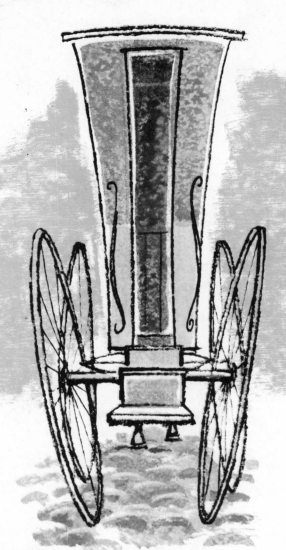

Then the old white horse
    went on down the street
    pulling the tall skinny wagon.

With its wiggly wheels squeaking,
    its body creaking,
    the horse's hoofs kept time:
        Clip—clop
        Clip—clop